D0466259

Little Miss Muffet

Trapani, Iza,
Little Miss Muffet /
[2013]
33305229382696
cu   04/04/14

Little Miss Muffet

As Told and Illustrated by Iza Trapani

Sky Pony Press
New York

≫⊸⊷ To my agent, Jennifer, who is wonderful and fearless! ⊶⊸≪

Copyright © 2013 by Iza Trapani

All rights reserved. No part of this book may be reproduced in any manner without the express written consent of the publisher, except in the case of brief excerpts in critical reviews or articles. All inquiries should be addressed to Sky Pony Press, 307 West 36th Street, 11th Floor, New York, NY 10018.

Sky Pony Press books may be purchased in bulk at special discounts for sales promotion, corporate gifts, fund-raising, or educational purposes. Special editions can also be created to specifications. For details, contact the Special Sales Department, Sky Pony Press, 307 West 36th Street, 11th Floor, New York, NY 10018 or info@skyhorsepublishing.com.

Sky Pony® is a registered trademark of Skyhorse Publishing, Inc.®, a Delaware corporation.

Visit our website at www.skyponypress.com.

10 9 8 7 6 5 4 3 2 1

Manufactured in China, May 2013
This product conforms to CPSIA 2008

Library of Congress Cataloging-in-Publication Data
is available on file.

ISBN: 978-1-62087-986-3

Little Miss Muffet
Sat on a tuffet,
Eating her curds and whey.
Along came a spider
Who sat down beside her
And frightened Miss Muffet away.

All through
the room,

She zipped and
she zoomed

And looked for a
place to hide.

A mouse came to find her;
It scurried behind her.
The dainty Miss bolted outside.

Next to the flowers,
She crouched for hours,
Scared of what she might see.

A frog leaped above her.
She dashed and took cover
Way up in the top of a tree.

Oh, she was dizzy,
In such a tizzy,
Looking below with dread.

A crow cackled near her.
She shrieked! Did you hear her?
Back down to the bottom she fled.

In her canoe,
She paddled out to
The middle of her big pond.

A fish jumped and stunned her.
Kerplunk! She went under,
Head-over-heels, upside down!

Quickly she scuttered
Out of the water,
Then had her biggest scare.

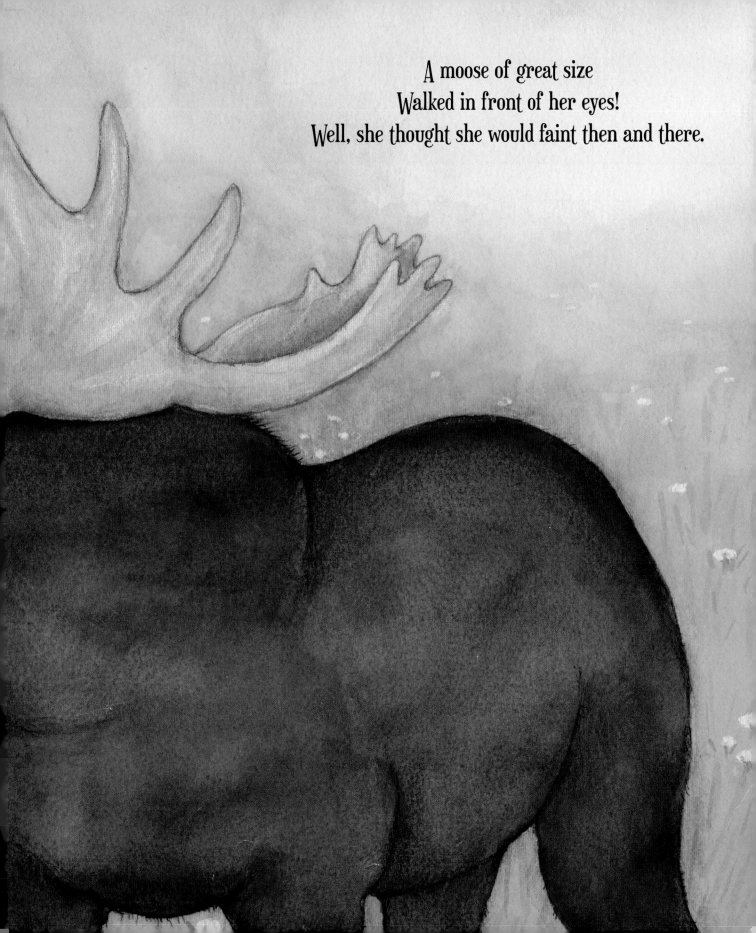

A moose of great size
Walked in front of her eyes!
Well, she thought she would faint then and there.

Over the hill,
She sprinted until
She made it to her front door.

Inside, she got tidy,
Then put on her nightie
And went to her tuffet once more.

Little Miss Muffet sat on a tuffet,
Eating her curds and whey.
The future looked bright—
Not a critter in sight.
She had had enough scares for one day.

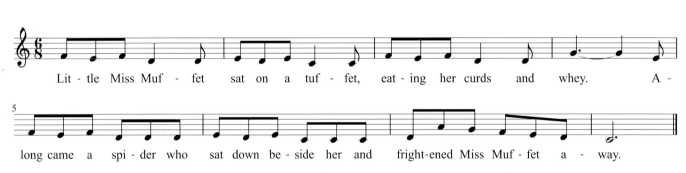

Lit-tle Miss Muf-fet sat on a tuf-fet, eat-ing her curds and whey. A-long came a spi-der who sat down be-side her and fright-ened Miss Muf-fet a-way.

2. All through the room,
She zipped and she zoomed,
And looked for a place to hide.
A mouse came to find her;
It scurried behind her.
The dainty Miss bolted outside.

3. Next to the flowers,
She crouched for hours,
Scared of what she might see.
A frog leaped above her.
She dashed and took cover
Way up in the top of a tree.

4. Oh, she was dizzy,
In such a tizzy,
Looking below with dread.
A crow cackled near her.
She shrieked! Did you hear her?
Back down to the bottom she fled.

5. In her canoe
She paddled out to
The middle of her big pond.
A fish jumped and stunned her.
Kerplunk! She went under,
Head-over-heels, upside down!

6. Quickly she scuttered,
Out of the water,
Then had her biggest scare.
A moose of great size
Walked in front of her eyes!
Well, she thought she would faint then
    and there.

7. Over the hill,
She sprinted until
She made it to her front door.
Inside, she got tidy,
Then put on her nightie,
And went to her tuffet once more.

8. Little Miss Muffet sat on a tuffet,
Eating her curds and whey.
The future looked bright—
Not a critter in sight.
She had had enough scares for one day.